A NOTE TO PARENTS

When your children are ready to "step into reading," giving them the right books is as crucial to their development as giving them the right food to eat. **Step into Reading®** books feature exciting stories and information reinforced with lively, colorful illustrations that make learning to read fun, satisfying, and rewarding. We have even taken *extra* steps to keep your child engaged by offering Step into Reading Sticker books, Step into Reading Math books, and Step into Reading Phonics books, in addition to fabulous fiction and nonfiction.

Learning to read, Step by Step:

- **Super Early** books (Preschool–Kindergarten) support pre-reading skills. Parent and child can engage in "see and say" reading using the strong picture cues and the few simple words on each page.
- **Early** books (Preschool–Kindergarten) let emergent readers tackle one or two short sentences of large type per page.
- **Step 1** books (Preschool–Grade 1) have the same easy-to-read type as Early, but with more words per page.
- **Step 2** books (Grades 1–3) offer longer and slightly more difficult text while introducing contractions and clauses. Children are often drawn to our exciting natural science nonfiction titles at this level.
- **Step 3** books (Grades 2–3) present paragraphs, chapters, and fully developed plot lines in fiction and nonfiction.
- **Step 4** books (Grades 2–4) feature thrilling nonfiction illustrated with exciting photographs for independent as well as reluctant readers.

Remember: The grade levels assigned to the six steps are intended only as guides. Some children move through all six steps rapidly; others climb the steps over a period of a few years. Either way, these books will help children "step into reading" for life!

To Carl
—M. M.

www.randomhouse.com/kids/disney

Library of Congress Cataloging-in-Publication Data
McVeigh, Mark, 1964–
Buzz vs. Torque: one on one / by Mark McVeigh.
    p. cm.—(Step into Reading; A step 2 book)
SUMMARY: Buzz Lightyear is about to be beaten by his enemy Torque, whose secret weapon is the ability to multiply himself at will.
ISBN 0-7364-1227-1 — ISBN 0-7364-8007-2 (lib. bdg.)
[1.Toys—Fiction.] I.Title: Buzz vs. Torque. II. Title. III. Step into Reading. Step 2 book.
PZ7.M2485 Bu 2001
[E]—dc21
2001019775

Printed in the United States of America   May 2002   10 9 8 7 6 5 4 3 2 1

STEP INTO READING, RANDOM HOUSE, and the Random House colophon are registered trademarks of Random House, Inc.

BUZZ vs. TORQUE:
one-on-one

A STEP 2 BOOK

By Mark McVeigh

Illustrated by Atelier Philippe Harchy

Random House New York

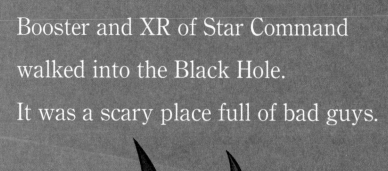

Booster and XR of Star Command
walked into the Black Hole.
It was a scary place full of bad guys.

But they had a job to do.

The Space Rangers
had to arrest a bad guy
named Torque.
Booster was excited.
XR just wanted to go home!

TORQUE
{ TORK }

Booster spotted Torque.

"You are under arrest," he said.

But Torque was always

ready for a fight.

No one was going to get *him*!

Booster was in trouble.
"If only Buzz Lightyear
were here," said XR.

Buzz *was* there!

And so was Mira.

Buzz zapped Torque's

laser gun.

Mira launched

an energy net at him.

The Space Rangers moved

in fast to arrest him.

"Four against one,"
Buzz said to Torque.
"You never had a chance."

Guardbots led Torque away.
A prison ship was waiting.
"I hope you like the Prison
Planet," said Buzz.

On the way
to the Prison Planet,
Hornets attacked the ship.
They kidnapped Torque!

The Hornets sped Torque
to Planet Z instead.
Evil Emperor Zurg
needed Torque to help him
with an evil plan.

Torque was led into
Zurg's throne room.
"I am going to give you
special powers," said Zurg.
"And then I want you
to get Buzz Lightyear."

Torque was scared.
But he *did* want
to get back at Buzz.
Zurg gave the signal.
Huge lasers zapped Torque!

When it was over,

Torque tested his new powers.

He thumped his chest plate.

One Torque . . .

turned into
two Torques . . .

turned into
three Torques!
It worked!

Zurg smiled an evil smile.

"Go get Buzz NOW!" he said.

Back in Tanker Alley,
the Space Rangers
were on safety duty.

They were fixing the buoys
that kept tankers
from crashing.

Space Ranger Rocket Crockett
flew up with bad news.
"The prison ship was attacked
by Hornets," said Rocket.
"Torque escaped!"

Buzz could not wait

to look for Torque.

He did not have to wait long.

Torque came looking for *him*!

"Hiya, Buzzy," said Torque.

Buzz took off after him.

He would fight Torque

one-on-one!

Or would he?

Buzz followed Torque.

When he landed, he saw

that Torque had multiplied!

Buzz counted *three* of him.

And more kept coming!

Buzz alone was no match
for this many bad guys!
Where were the other
Space Rangers
when he needed them?

They were in Tanker Alley,
still fixing safety buoys.
Mira, Booster, and XR
were worried.
Buzz had been missing
for hours.

All of a sudden,
many Torques attacked!

They tied the Space Rangers
to a runaway fuel tanker.
"When Buzz comes back,
you will be sorry," said XR.

"Oh, yeah?" said a Torque.

Two Torques slammed Buzz

onto the tanker.

They tied *him* down, too.

Buzz was out cold!

The tanker was speeding
right for Capital Planet.
"Leaping lasers!" said Booster.
"We have to do something!"

Luckily,

each of the Space Rangers

had a special power.

Mira slipped out of the bonds

like a ghost.

XR cut himself free with a laser.

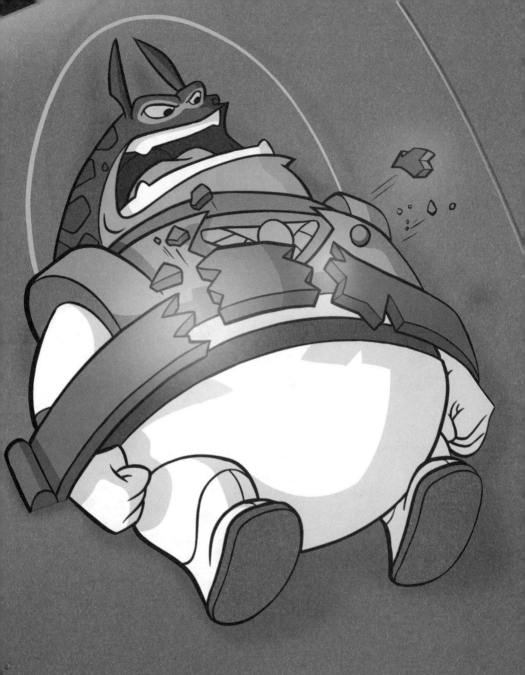

Booster broke free

with his huge muscles.

Mira checked the tanker's
steering and brakes.
They were broken!

Booster shook Buzz awake.
"Wake up, Buzz!" he said.
"Capital Planet is toast
if this tanker hits!"

Buzz got an idea—

the safety buoys!

He jetted back to Tanker Alley.

The others followed.

One by one, they grabbed buoys.

The Space Rangers
put the buoys in place.

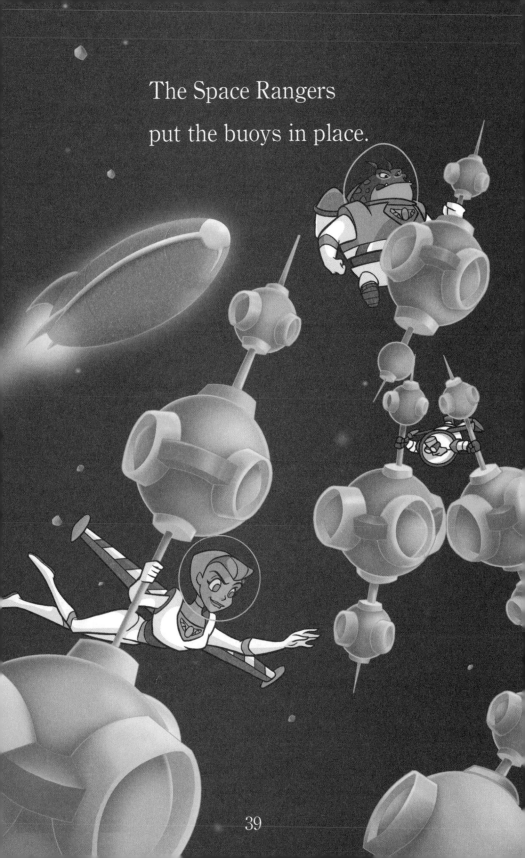

They made a path leading
away from Capital Planet.
The tanker ran into a buoy
and bounced off into space.
Capital Planet was safe.
"We did it!" shouted Buzz.

But there was still one problem—
or was it two or three?
It was time to track down
the army of Torques.
The Space Rangers headed
back to the Black Hole.

The Torques were all there.
"You boys sure seem happy,"
said Buzz.
"But not for long."

Space Rangers filled the room.

"*We* outnumber *you*!" said Mira.

"Take them, Rangers!" yelled Buzz.

It was a big battle.
But the Space Rangers
worked together.

Every Torque was rounded up.
Guardbots led them all onto
the prison ship.

The Torques were *chained* together this time!

"Today is Torque's lucky day,"
said Buzz.

"I hear the Prison Planet
is offering a group discount!"
Buzz and his Space Rangers
headed for Star Command.

"To infinity and beyond!"